World of Reading

STAR WARS™

TRAPPED IN THE DEATH STAR!

WRITTEN BY MICHAEL SIGLAIN

ART BY PILOT STUDIO

DISNEP
LUCASFILM
PRESS
Los Angeles • New York

Printed in China

First Boxed Set Edition, July 2017   10 9 8 7 6 5 4 3 2 1

Library of Congress Control Number on file

FAC-025393-17104

ISBN 978-1-368-01495-3

Visit the official *Star Wars* website at: www.starwars.com.

The dreaded Death Star floated
in the far reaches of space.

The Death Star was a
fearsome space station.
It was as big as a moon.
It could destroy planets.

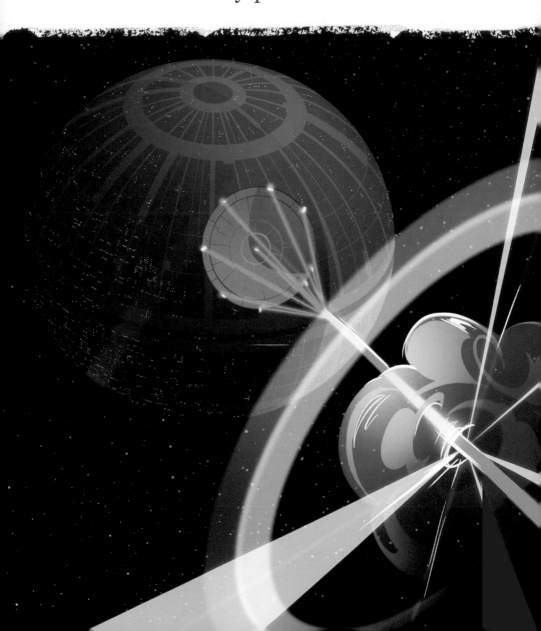

A man named Tarkin was
in charge of the Death Star.
Tarkin worked with the
evil lord Darth Vader.
Tarkin and Vader wanted
to rule the galaxy.

Luke and Ben wanted
to save the galaxy.
Ben was a Jedi Knight.
He was training Luke.
Han and Chewie were helping them.
They were all flying in Han's ship.

Han's ship was captured
by the Death Star!
The heroes hid in Han's ship.
No one found them.

Han and Luke put on
stormtrooper armor.
They had to turn off the machine
that captured Han's ship.

Luke's droid R2-D2
read the Death Star's computer.
R2-D2 learned that Princess Leia
was also on the Death Star.
Luke and Han had to save her!

Luke and Han pretended
to be troopers.
They fought against the
real troopers.

Luke found the princess.
They needed to escape!

But the heroes were trapped.
Princess Leia had an idea.
She blasted a hole in the wall.
The heroes jumped through the hole . . .

. . . and into a pile
of smelly garbage!

The troopers knew the
heroes were in the garbage.
The troopers started closing
the walls on the heroes!

The heroes were going
to be crushed!

Luke called the droids for help.

R2-D2 and C-3PO
stopped the walls from closing.
The heroes were saved!

But they were still trapped in
the Death Star.
And they were still on the run from
the troopers.

Han and Chewie chased the troopers!

Then the troopers chased
Han and Chewie!

Luke and Leia were also on the run.
They needed to get
back to Han's ship.
But they were stuck!
Luke had an idea.

Luke used a rope from his belt.

Luke and Leia swung to safety!

But the heroes were *still* trapped
in the Death Star.
Only old Ben could save them.

Ben turned off the machine.
Now Han's ship could leave!

The heroes met back at Han's ship.
But the heroes could not get to the ship.
The troopers were guarding it.

Ben could not get to the ship, either.
Darth Vader was in his way.

Darth Vader and Ben fought!

Darth Vader struck Ben.

But Ben was no longer there.

Ben had become one with the Force.

The troopers were watching
Darth Vader.
They were not watching the heroes.
The heroes ran to Han's ship!

Han's ship flew away from
the Death Star.
The heroes had finally escaped!

But Tarkin and Vader would not rest
until they ruled the galaxy!